In Truth,
It's All About
The Baby

Shirley Farley & Billie Stultz

illustrated by Shirley

Written by Shirley Farley & Billie Stultz

Illustrations by Shirley Farley

Scripture taken from the *New King James Version®*. © 1982 by Thomas Nelson. Used by permission. All rights reserved. (NKJV)

Scripture taken from *The Holy Bible, King James Version*. Cambridge Edition: 1769; *King James Bible Online*, 2022. www.kingjamesbibleonline.org. (KJV)

Scripture taken from *THE HOLY BIBLE, NEW INTERNATIONAL VERSION®*, NIV® Copyright © 1973, 1978, 1984, 2011 by Biblica, Inc.® Used by permission. All rights reserved worldwide. (NIV)

Copyright © 2022 by SGBLit, Inc
All rights reserved under International and Pan-American Copyright Conventions. This book or any portion thereof may not be reproduced or used in any manner whatsoever without the express written permission of the publisher except for the use of brief quotations in a book review.

ISBN – 979-8-98-655370-2

Published by: YesBear Publishing

Authors available for speaking

CONTACT INFO:
www.SGBLit.com
billie@sgblit.com
shirley@sgblit.com

Forward

This is a work of fiction. The Part I stories and characters are mostly from my imagination and are woven into the scripture stories. Even in their short stories, these characters became real to me and mostly wrote their own stories.

I hope you enjoy these stories. Even though some of the stories are a bit difficult to hear, there is always hope when you find Jesus.

The companion stories in Part II, "Dutimus," "Sozo's Tale," "Bemacheval," "Dutimus and the Baby Boy, Jesus," and "Naba" were written by my sister, Billie Stultz, to go along with the other stories in Part I. I believe these stories are a fun telling of the animal's tales about the birth of Jesus. After all, all of nature has it in it to praise God.

Shirley Farley

Dedication

We dedicate this book to our mother, Alma Cleo Farley. Her love, support, and the push to always draw our own conclusions has helped us become the women we are today. We are stronger, more loving, caring, and thoughtful than we could ever have been on our own. We love you Mom, and are unbelievably blessed to be your daughters.

Shirley, Gail, & Billie

We would also like to say thank you for the help we received along the way:

The inspiration and guidance of the Holy Spirit - whom we pray that we honor in all that we do

Many amazing and dedicated leaders serving through Sunday School, sermons, Bible studies, pod casts and personal reading who helped us gain knowledge of the Holy Scriptures

Gail, our sister, who has always been a stabilizing force in our lives, for lending us her stellar proof-reading skills, offering advice and encouragement throughout this process, and agreeing to serve as our business manager

Billie's husband Jim and their children who help keep her grounded and well-loved

Mark, Gail's husband and our beloved brother, who interrupts his own work to call out an amazing myriad

of advice and information just when it is needed—
including pinch hitting the creation of our SBGLit
logo

Steve Young of Yes Bear Publishing, who helped get
the book to print and patiently fielded our 1,001
questions

Many friends who read portions of the book and
provided feedback and encouragement, especially
Shirley's Sunday School Class, Women of the Word

Mark Rathjen, who read, advised, encouraged, and
critiqued Shirley's writing

Carolyn Searcy and Jeff LeJeune, Billie's friends, for
their encouragement of her writing

Favorite ministries Billie studies which have helped
her grow, challenged her, and expanded her spiritual
understanding

Contents

Part I

"What Child Is This?
The Eyewitness Stories

The characters in these stories are all mentioned or suggested in Jesus' birth story. From the shepherds who saw the angels, to the innkeeper who had no rooms, to the soldiers sent to kill the baby Jesus, each encountered or were affected by the birth of Jesus. Their stories here are my imaginings of how that encounter might have changed each person, for I believe that anytime someone has an encounter with Jesus that they are changed. It is up to each person to decide how to respond and each person has a choice to make.   Read their stories and decide for yourself if you think this is how they might have been touched and changed.   Be prepared as you read to possibly have an encounter yourself and think about how you might have responded in their places.

Shirley Farley

Chapter 1

The Old Shepherd
I Saw the Angels

Luke 2:8-18

The old Shepherd sat near the fire, grief etched on his weathered face. His grandsons sat nearby, not knowing what to say or how to comfort him. The sheep were all lying nearby at peace and protected for the night. These were good shepherds and they knew how to keep their sheep safe.

The younger shepherds watched tears roll down their grandfather's face. They were shocked, dismayed. Shepherds were known for being stoic, hiding their hurts and disappointments well. After all, they were among the most looked down upon of their people. They were considered dirty, poor, uneducated, and men who were good for nothing other than to guard someone's sheep. They had learned from an early age to hide their feelings, even from each other. Yet, here was their grandfather, leader of their clan, crying openly. They were frightened by it and wanted to ask why, yet were not sure that they wanted to know.

Then, as they watched, the Grandfather's face changed. It seemed to take on a glow, and a look of awe replaced the tears. Now they were really shaken. Grandfather was old, in his sixties. Very old for a man at that time, and yet just yesterday, he had seemed to be as strong and healthy as any of them. Was he losing his mind; was he dying? What should they do?

Finally, one of the grandsons spoke up and asked, "Grandfather, are you ok?"

The old shepherd sat for a few moments without answering and then said, "Yes, my grandsons. I have a story to tell you."

"Thirty-three years ago, when I was younger than even some

of you, I saw something that changed my life forever. I was on a hillside near Bethlehem with a group of shepherds. It was a very cold night, and we were all huddled around the campfire, trying to stay warm while still keeping watch over our flocks. We were joking, talking, trying to stay warm and awake through the night. I think old Simeon even brought out his flute so that we could sing."

The old shepherd stopped speaking for a moment lost in thought about that night long ago.

"It was a very dark night, no moon, just the stars overhead. Then suddenly, the sky lit up as if someone had just turned on the sun. It was brighter than daylight. An angel of the Lord, yes, a real angel, stood next to us, and we saw that the light was the glory of the Lord shining on us. We were terrified. I am pretty sure I cried and tried to hide my face. Then the angel spoke to us. It really spoke to us. A poor, dirty group of shepherds that no one would ever have taken the time of day for, and one of God's very angels spoke to us!"

One of the grandsons asked in awe, "What did it say, Grandfather?" They had heard the story before but never like this.

The Old Shepherd replied, "It said, 'Do not be afraid. I bring you good news that will cause great joy for all the people' "

(Luke 2:10 NIV).

The Grandfather paused and shook his head. "Can you imagine God choosing to send His angel to a group of shepherds to share the news that would bring joy to all people? It was unthinkable, and yet it did happen just as I am telling you."

Then the angel said, "Today in the town of David a Savior has been born to you; he is the Messiah, the Lord. This will be a sign to you: You will find a baby wrapped in cloths and lying in a manger" (Luke 2:11-12 NIV).

"Then suddenly the whole sky was filled with angels. They were praising God and saying, 'Glory to God in the highest, on earth peace, good will toward men' " (Luke 2:14 KJV).

"They were there for a while, and then they were gone. Oh, how dark the night seemed after that heavenly light and the angels withdrew."

Then, one by one, we shepherds stood up and said, "Let's go to Bethlehem right now and see this baby that the Lord has told us about."

"We all left our sheep, something you know we never do. Why, even today, if there were an emergency at least one of us would stay to defend our flocks."

"But that night, that glorious night, we all just stood up and left. No one wanted to be left out of seeing God's greatest gift to man."

"We marched right into Bethlehem and, after some searching, found the stable. And there was the baby, just as the angel told us. He was wrapped up tightly in strips of cloth and lying in a feeding trough. His mother was there and smiled when she saw us. Joseph, her husband, was also there protecting mother and child. I think he may have been slightly alarmed at a group of dirty, smelly shepherds suddenly staring down at the little boy, but Mary, the mother, just smiled. We told them about the angels and what they said, and we worshipped that child, the Savior that God had promised many, many years ago."

"And then we left to return to our sheep, praising God as we went. We told many, many people about that night. Some were amazed and others skeptical, but we never stopped talking about that night. We could not. How could we keep such joyful news that was for all people to ourselves?"

Ponder—Read Luke 2:8-18

- The story says that shepherds were looked down upon during the time of the birth of Jesus. Why might this have been? How are shepherds viewed today? Do you know anyone who is a shepherd? Is there any group of people you look down upon because of their profession?

- Why do you think God chose to reveal the birth of His Son to a group of shepherds and not to important religious people or leaders of their nation?

- What is an angel?

- How did the shepherds feel when the angel arrived? How would feel if an angel suddenly appeared in front of you?

- Do you believe that angels are real? Why or why not?

- Why did the shepherds tell everyone about what they had seen and heard? Do you think you would have believed them?

- Do you think the shepherds were changed by the visit from the angel and seeing the baby? If so, how were they changed?

My Conclusions

The old shepherd had an experience of divine revelation from God. He was changed the night the angels appeared to him. His understanding and belief of what he knew of God and the prophecies taught to him, as they were to all Hebrew boys, became stronger as he grew older.

The Innkeeper
No Rooms Here

Luke 2:6-7

W hat a crazy year this has been! The census has kept all of us running. Of course, it means that my budget is made for next year. My accounts are full, and my taxes are paid up. Maybe I can even afford to build a real stable, draw in some more affluent guests. Speaking of that lean-to for the animals that I call a stable, it sure has seen some strange sights this year. I don't understand all that happened, but it seems to have been almost miraculous. Hmmm, maybe I should keep that stable as is, just in case that baby becomes famous. I could charge people to see it. It is just an idea."

"But maybe something special did happen there. It all started several weeks ago."

I remember thinking, "Here comes another latecomer looking for a place to stay! Well, they'll find out just like all the others that there is not a bed or place to sleep anywhere in Bethlehem. I even have two strangers sleeping on the floor of my chambers, and they paid good money for it!"

The couple, yes, it was a couple, approached my door. The young woman was riding on a donkey, and she did not look well. Then I saw she was quite big with child. Why in the world would this man bring his young, very pregnant wife on this journey with him? Couldn't she have just stayed with some of their family? It was not necessary for her to register in the census; her husband could do that for the whole family. Didn't he trust her, or she him? Or maybe they just wanted to be together for what was going to be their first child. Whatever their reason, it didn't seem like such a good idea to me. She was obviously in some distress.

The man spoke. "I'm Joseph ,and this is my wife, Mary. We have come from Nazareth for the census. We've looked everywhere for a place to stay."

Mary suddenly moaned. She grasped Joseph's arm and said, "Hurry. It's almost time."

Joseph turned pale. He turned to me quickly and said, "Please tell us you have a place for us to stay."

I panicked a little myself. Was this young woman going to give birth right on my doorstep? How would that look for business?

"I'm sorry," I said, "but I am full to overflowing too. There are no rooms left in Bethlehem!"

Mary moaned again ,and I panicked even more. I had to get rid of them. But something about that young woman captured my sympathy. I couldn't even give them my room since I already had two strangers sleeping there. I didn't think they would appreciate a pregnant woman giving birth while they were trying to sleep.

Then I thought about the old stable behind the inn. It wasn't much, but it did have a roof and walls. And the stable-hand had just mucked it out today, so it was as clean as it could be. I had to get them off my doorstep before that baby showed up!

So I turned to Joseph and told him about the stable and that they were welcome to stay there.

Joseph did not look too happy or excited, but Mary whispered to him, and he accepted my offer. I hurriedly showed them the way to the stable and then went back to check on my paying guests.

Later that evening, I went out to check on them. There was an unusually bright star shining that night. I didn't even need a lantern to light my way to the stable. It was quite late, but my curiosity got the better of me. I sure hoped that young woman was all right. When I got to that stable, a strange sight met my eyes. The baby had been born. It was wrapped up and lying in one of the feeding troughs. Mary was sitting nearby, resting, and a whole group of shepherds was standing there looking in awe at that baby.

Where had they come from? Were they related to the couple? Where were their sheep? What in the world was going on? I just stood back in the shadows and watched. Finally, the shepherds took their leave. As they were going, I heard them speaking.

"It is just like the angel said. The baby was exactly where it said it would be. The Lord Most High has blessed us greatly in seeing His promised savior."

What were they saying? Angels, savior, blessed by God? Had they all lost their minds? But they seemed so sure, so excited, so—blessed.

They continued talking excitedly as they headed back toward the hills and their sheep.

I peeked in at the baby, and the young mother saw me and smiled. I smiled back and then returned to my inn.

Sometime later that year, something even stranger happened. By that time, Joseph and Mary had moved into a nearby house. I kept my eye on them as I had taken a shine to Mary and the little boy, who called me "Unc" for uncle.

The house was not much, but even I had to admit it was better than my lean-to. I helped with leftovers and other things as I could. After all, it had been a very lucrative year for me thanks to that census that drew so many people here.

I looked down the street and saw three richly dressed men entering their little house. Not being able to help myself and wanting to be sure that all was well with the little family, I strolled down the street to their house. Who knew? Maybe those three men might need a nice, cozy inn room in which to stay. The least I could do was offer them my hospitality.

I peeked through a crack in the door and saw those three men bow down to Jesus, the little boy. "How strange," I thought. Then as I watched, each brought out a rich gift, gifts fit for a king, and presented them to the little boy. I really hoped at that point that they wanted a room for a prolonged stay!

It was as bright outside as it was inside that little house, and I swear that Mary saw me peeking in and winked at me. Embarrassed at being caught, I hurried back toward my inn. That was the last time I saw those three rich men and the last time I saw that little family.

The next day, when I went to check on the family, the house was empty. They were gone. They did not even say goodbye. They were there when I went to bed and gone the next morning. I was a little miffed, I must say, that they didn't even bother to come and tell me goodbye and thank me. Someone said they saw them leaving in the middle of the night, but they were not on the road headed back to Nazareth. They were on the road leading toward Egypt. I didn't believe that. Just idle gossip, I am sure. Why would that young couple have gone to Egypt —— no friends, no family there? Probably not even a friendly, generous innkeeper like me.

A short time later, I was glad that the little family had left. A group of soldiers came through Bethlehem and murdered every little boy under two years old. It would have broken my heart if that family had been harmed.

That is the end of my story tonight. Don't believe it? Well, those shepherds are up there in those hills. They come into town every once in a while and tell anyone who will listen about the angels and the baby born in my stable. Many others saw those three wise men. And you don't have to ask about the killing of those babies. All you have to do is look and listen to the ever-present wailing of those children's grief- stricken parents.

Who was that baby? I don't know, but he had to be some kind of special, that I do know. I would love to meet him all grown up someday and hear the rest of his story. It must be something.

Ponder—Read Luke 2:6-7

- The innkeeper was a businessman. Was he wrong in looking to make a profit for his business?

- Is making money the only reason to start a business? What might be some other reasons to start a business?

- Do you think the innkeeper could or should have made money showing people the stable where Jesus was born? Why or Why not?

- The innkeeper was a witness to many things in this

story. Do you think he believed what he was seeing? Do you think he understood what he saw and heard? Why or why not?

- Have you ever questioned who Jesus was or is?

- Do you think that the innkeeper had a decision to make?

- Did he need more information to make his decision? If so, what information did he need?

- Have you made a decision about Jesus? If so, what did you need to know to make your decision?

My Conclusions

The innkeeper was a businessman. In the beginning of his story, he seemed to look at everything that happened because of that baby boy as a potential profit. Yet, as he continued sharing all that he had seen and heard, he began to wonder just who that baby really was. In the end, he had questions, and one has to hope someone met him and told him the rest of the story as the baby grew up and became a man. He had a choice to make, but he needed more information.

Chapter 3

The Magi
Who Are We?

Matthew 2:1-12; Daniel 2:46-49

My name is Melchior, and I am the oldest and, therefore, chief of the Magi. So few people understand who we are. They see us as mystics, wise men from the East, and so we are, but we are so much more. We are trained astronomers and know how to read the movement of the stars and the planets in the sky. We are able to interpret dreams, and we know about the God of the Hebrews and His prophecies concerning a coming Messiah, a savior for the Jewish people, and we believe, also for the rest of the world.

How do we know this Jewish tradition? Well, that answer is simple. Many generations earlier, a young Hebrew man came to Babylonia as a slave, but during his time there, he was made the chief over all the practicing wise men and Magi of that region. His name was Daniel, but our tradition knows him better as Belteshazzar, the name he was given when he arrived in Babylonia.[1]

Belteshazzar was a strong believer in the One True God of his people, the Jews. He was wise beyond his years when he arrived in Babylon and soon caught the eye of the men over him. When King Nebuchadnezzar had a troubling dream, he called on all his priests, sorcerers, and wise men to explain his dream to him. However, as troubled as the king was, he did not trust his priests and wise men. So he did not demand just an explanation of the meaning of the dream; he demanded

---

[1] Abbott, Shari. "How Did the Wise Men (Magi) Know This Was the Messiah? How Did They Know to Follow His Star?" *Reasons for Hope* Jesus*, 2022, reasonsforhopejesus.com/wise-men-still-follow-his-star/.

them to tell him what his dream was and then interpret it. That was unheard of, and none of those "wise men" was able to do it. Those wise men were scared and told the king that what he demanded was impossible, it had never been done, and only the gods who did not live among flesh could do such a thing. Therefore, the king ordered all the wise men to be killed, including Daniel and some of his Hebrew friends. When Daniel heard why they were to be slain. he requested some time from the king, and then he and his Hebrew friends sought the mercies of their God. God revealed the dream and its meaning to Daniel. Daniel was rushed to the king before all the wise men were killed and he told the king about his dream and its interpretation. Daniel explained no man could do what the king had asked, but there was a God in heaven who revealed secrets. The king was so impressed with Daniel and his God that he chose Daniel to rule over the whole of Babylon and put him over all the wise men. Since Daniel was now the chief wise man, he shared his faith with us. Many wise men believed in Daniel's God and passed on Daniel's teachings throughout our generations. Later, Daniel also served among the Medes and the Persians, of which we three wise men come. We follow the God of Daniel and watch for his revelations in the sky.

"It is happening," my friend and fellow Magi, Caspar, rushed in to tell me.

“What is happening?” I demanded.

“The star that Belteshazzar told us about has risen. It is time. The savior of the Jews has been born,” he continued.

We both ran outside to study the night sky. Sure enough, there was a bright new star in the sky. It seemed to be looking at us as if it were waiting on us. Now that was a surprise!

About that time, Balthasar came out, and we all stood gazing at the sky until dawn.

“What shall we do?” I asked.

One of my two friends and fellow Magi replied, “We must follow that star and go worship the newborn king and savior of whom Belteshazzar told us. Remember, there are some specific gifts that we are to take and give to this new king. We had better hurry and prepare for this trip because it is a long way from here to Israel. It will take us many days to get there.”

And so we began our preparations. We prayed and worshipped the One True God and then began gathering the things that would be necessary for our long journey.

Now I will admit that I was no longer a young man, and I was not looking forward to a long trip on the back of a camel. Have you ever ridden a camel? I promise you it is not the most comfortable way to get anywhere. You are constantly swaying and must pay attention so you do not fall off. If you are prone to seasickness, it will get you every time on a camel. Why do you think they are called the 'ships of the desert?' But there was no way, as chief of the Magi, that I was not going to go and worship this gift from God.

Finally, after several weeks of preparation, we started on our journey. How did we know where to go? We followed that star that sat still in the sky during our preparations as if it were waiting on us, but the moment we got on our camels, it began slowly moving in front of us. Surely this could only be by the providence of Daniel's and our God.

Finally, after many, many long, tiring weeks, we arrived in Jerusalem. We went immediately to the palace to ask where the new king was to be born. Strange as it was, we were taken directly into the presence of King Herod. When he realized we were Magi from the East, he sought our wisdom about this newborn king since none of his people had recognized the signs. He asked us about the star we had followed. Then he demanded of his religious leaders where this baby was to be born, and, after consulting their prophetical writings, they revealed that the baby was to be born in Bethlehem.

Then King Herod told us, "Go and search diligently for the young child; and when ye have found *him*, bring me word again, that I may come and worship him also" (Matthew 2:8

KJV).

We took our leave of King Herod, eager to get to Bethlehem. As we left Jerusalem, the star continued to move before us, and we followed.

Arriving in Bethlehem, we wandered through the town until we came to a little house, and there was our star sitting over it, a beacon calling to us. We found a nearby place to leave our camels, gathered up our gifts, and knocked on the door of the house glowing in the light of our star.

A man came to the door and looked at us with curiosity and suspicion. We told him that we were Magi come from the East and that we had followed the star of the newborn king of the Jews to this house. He looked startled but opened the door for us to enter the house. His wife came to stand beside him. When she heard us tell about the star, she poked her head out and smiled at it.

She invited us in and introduced her husband to us as Joseph and herself as Mary. Then we saw the little boy. He was no longer a baby. He was walking and talking a little. Mary told us his name was Jesus.

We bowed down before the child. He just stood there and smiled at us. No crying because three strangers had entered his home, no fear etched on his little face, just a smile as he looked at us.

We explained that we had come from very far away to worship this promise from God and that we had gifts for the child. We brought out the gifts that Daniel had told us to take when the time came.

First, Caspar brought out the gold and laid it at the child's feet. The little boy looked at it but then went back to playing with a small ball. His parents looked on in shock at the richness of the gold before them.

Then, Balthasar brought out a large bottle of frankincense, a very costly scent. Sometimes it was even used to anoint kings when they were buried.

Then it was my turn. I bought out a bottle of myrrh, another costly perfume. This perfume was used to anoint the high priest as he performed his priestly duties.

The parent's eyes grew bigger with each gift, but the mother also looked very thoughtful. Somehow, the gifts seemed appropriate, even if they were given to a toddler.

We stayed for a while longer, visiting and worshipping the child, and then we headed out of town. While we slept that night, we had a dream, a vision from God. He warned us not to return to King Herod because Herod was seeking to kill the child. We knew this to be a true dream, as we all had the same dream. So we took a different route to return home. We did not see King Herod again, nor did we see that child again, but we did follow what happened to him. It was all as Daniel had told us it would be, and even now, we continue to worship the One True God and thank Him for the blessing we received while worshipping the Savior.

We also heard about what Herod did in ordering those baby boys killed, all born from the time we first saw the star up through two years old. Oh, how we regretted going to see Herod, but we also knew that this was part of the prophecy about the coming savior. We thanked God for warning us and for protecting His child from Herod.

This is our story. We are not magicians or astrologers, as some have claimed. We are worshippers of the One True God, the God of Israel, the Creator of the world. Our wisdom and knowledge come from Him and only Him.

Ponder—Read Matthew 2:1-12 and Daniel 2:1-49

- How much do you know about the Magi? You may want to research who and what they were. Their history is fascinating.

- Did you know about the Daniel of the Lion's Den story and that Daniel was made the chief of all the different types of wise men in Babylon? Can you explain how that happened?

- Why was Daniel's name changed to Belteshazzar? Do you know someone whose name was changed? Why was it changed?

- Do you think the Magi made a mistake in going to Herod? Why or why not?

- The Magi said they knew that what Herod did was a part of prophecy concerning the coming savior. Find this particular prophecy and read about it.

- There are many other prophecies about the coming savior in the Old Testament. Find two and describe the prophecies.

- Can you find how these prophecies were fulfilled during Jesus' lifetime?

My Conclusions

The Magi were prophets, mystics who had been taught to watch for the birth of a new King of the Jews. They understood God's prophecies of many years before and knew their kind had been waiting since the days of the prophet Daniel. They had no questions, only sure convictions that the star foretold the birth and that they had to go and see the new king. Their only misstep might be that they went to Herod to discover where the newborn king was to be found. Of course, even their trip to Herod was a part of God-given prophecies concerning the promised Savior coming true. They followed a star to the baby Jesus, worshipped, and gifted him, and then returned to their home country. It is certain that they shared with others in their home country about how the king and savior had been born.

Joseph
Me, the One to Raise God's Son?

Matthew 1:18-25; 2:13-14

I looked over at Mary and the little boy riding on the donkey as we secretly left Bethlehem in the middle of the night. The donkey carried not only our little boy but also our few possessions, including the precious gifts from the three Magi who had presented them to Jesus. I was very grateful for those gifts. I knew that we were going to need them to survive in Egypt.

I hated leaving secretly in the middle of the night. I especially hated not being able to thank the innkeeper who had become like a family member during our time in Bethlehem. Jesus even called him Unc for uncle. It was, however, necessary that we leave quickly and in secret, for God had warned me in a dream that very night that King Herod was going to try to kill Jesus. God had spoken to me in a dream before, and I knew this was also a true dream. So we snuck out of town and headed to Egypt, where God told me to go. I was not excited about going to Egypt. We did not know anyone there or anything about Egypt. We Jewish people were still not very fond of Egypt, remembering the 400 years of slavery of our people there.

I know that God has been fulfilling His prophecies about the boy. There was a prophecy spoken by the prophet Hosea that said, I "called my son out of Egypt" (Hosea 11:1 KJV).

So here we were, sneaking out of Bethlehem and headed to

Egypt.

As I looked at Mary, I thought back to that night, almost two years ago, when we first arrived in Bethlehem. Mary was riding on the donkey then too, and she was so big with child that she looked ready to burst. It was obvious that she was not doing well; she was in pain and had been for a few hours. I worried that she was going to give birth to the baby right there on the back of the donkey in the wilderness before we ever reached Bethlehem. Thank Yahweh, we arrived in Bethlehem before the baby arrived.

Mary, my young, beautiful, sweet wife, smiled at me. She said, "We are ok, Joseph. Don't worry so much. God will take care of us!"

"Easy for you to say," I thought, "but I'm the one responsible for us."

Bethlehem was not a large town, but as we entered it at dusk, it was bustling. The streets were filled with people. Many others had also come to register for the census. We began going from inn to inn looking for a place to stay, but each time we were turned away . All the inns were full.

As we approached the last inn, I prayed, "Please, God, let us find a room here."

The innkeeper himself was standing at the door as we approached, shaking his head from side to side, but I kept on going towards him anyway.

"I'm Joseph and this is my wife, Mary. Please tell us that you have a place for us to stay tonight," I begged the innkeeper. About that time, Mary moaned, and I turned pale. The innkeeper looked closely at Mary for the first time, and he looked worried.

"I'm sorry," the innkeeper said, "but I am full to overflowing and so are all the other places to stay. I have no room here."

Mary moaned again, and the innkeeper looked rather sick himself. He seemed to panic as he realized Mary was about to give birth right there on his doorstep.

He looked at me and said, "It isn't much, but I have a stable out back. It has a roof and walls. It was just cleaned out today. You are welcome to stay there if you wish."

I was not too excited about my pregnant wife giving birth in a stable, no matter how clean it was, and was getting ready to refuse the offer when Mary grabbed my arm and whispered to me.

"It's time, Joseph. The baby is coming. The stable is fine, please!"

So we followed the innkeeper to the stable. It was clean and smelled good, like fresh straw. There was a well right next to it, and I was able to draw water for the coming baby and us.

We had a beautiful baby boy a while later, and Mary was doing surprisingly well. I washed the baby, and Mary wrapped him up tightly in strips of cloth, as is our tradition. Then we laid him in one of the clean mangers to sleep.

We both rested and ate the food that the kind innkeeper had sent out to us.

Late that night, we heard a commotion outside the stable. The door was pushed open, and there stood a group of shepherds looking in at us.

"Oh, no," I thought, "please tell me that we aren't going to have to share this stable with a bunch of shepherds."

But those shepherds just entered quietly, some kneeling and others standing respectfully, all looking at our baby boy in awe.

Then they told us their story, and it was quite a story. If I had not known just who our baby was, I would have thought they had all gotten into something intoxicating.

They told about an angel suddenly appearing to them and announcing the birth of the savior of the world. The angel said to them, "Fear not: for, behold, I bring you good tidings of great joy, which shall be to all people. For unto you is born this day in the city of David, a Savior, which is Christ the Lord. And this shall be a sign unto you; Ye shall find the babe wrapped in swaddling clothes, lying in a manger" (Luke 2:10-12 KJV).

Then they said the sky was filled with angels praising God and saying, "Glory to God in the highest, and on earth peace, good will toward men" (Luke 2:14 KJV).

"So," they said, "We all got up and came directly here to see this miracle, the promised one of God."

They visited a little longer and then returned to their flocks.

Mary and I sat in amazement throughout that night, thinking about all that had come about thus far with our little boy. After that night, we fulfilled all our religious obligations for the birth of a baby boy, and then we returned to Bethlehem and moved into a little house near our friend, the innkeeper. We stayed there for almost two years.

Then, just last night, there was a knock on our door. I opened it to the strangest sight. Three richly dressed strangers were standing on our doorstep, and an exceedingly bright star was shining down on our house. I just stood there staring at them with the door open when Mary came up beside me. The three men told us they were Magi from far away in the East and that they had followed the star above our house to see the new king of the Jews.

I saw Mary poke her head out the door, look up at that star, and smile. Then she turned to the three strangers and invited them into our home as she introduced us to them. I might have been standing there just staring at them for much longer if it had not been for Mary.

Those three strangers bowed down to Jesus when they saw him. Jesus just smiled at them and kept playing with the little ball that Unc, our innkeeper friend, had given him. About that time, I saw Mary wink at the door. I had no idea what that was about, but before I could question her, the three Magi began bringing out gifts fit for a king.

The first one put a pile of gold in front of Jesus. It was more money than I would ever see at one time during my life. The second one brought out a large bottle of frankincense, a very costly perfume. The third one brought out a bottle of Myrrh, probably worth as much as the first two gifts combined. I just stared in astonishment. Mary seemed to take it in stride.

The three visited for a while longer and then took their leave. We went to bed soon after, and that is when I had the dream telling us to go to Egypt. So here we are, fleeing Bethlehem and heading to Egypt.

The three of us, our meager belongings, one little donkey, and gifts fit for a king. I knew that those gifts would help us survive while we were hiding out in Egypt. I do not know how long we will need to be in Egypt, but I am sure God will call us back to Israel one day. After all, we are the caretakers of His most precious gift to Israel and the world, and as the prophets have written, Jesus will have a calling to fulfill for the Lord in Israel.

Ponder—Read Matthew 1:18-25; 2:13-14

- Who was Joseph? Who was his ancestor? Why is this important?

- Joseph had two dreams in which God gave him messages. What were those dreams?

- Have you ever had dreams that revealed something to you?

- Do you think people still have those dreams with messages from God today?

- How did Joseph show that he cared for Mary? For Jesus?

- Do you think that Joseph made a good father and husband? Why or Why not?

- Why was Joseph happy about the gifts from the Magi? What do you think he did with those gifts?

- How did the innkeeper come to be called Unc?

- Did Joseph know who Jesus was? How do you know this?

My Conclusions

Then, there was Joseph. As a Hebrew man, Joseph would have been taught the prophecies of the coming savior of the Jewish people. He would have believed in the prophecies but never expected to play a part in them himself. How hurt must he have been when Joseph first heard that Mary was pregnant. Yet, he was kind and cared enough that he did not plan to humiliate her publicly, but he planned to put aside the marriage in private. Then he had a prophetic dream that changed the course of the rest of his life. He was told that Mary was carrying the child of the Most High God and that he should marry her and take care of her. And he did just as he was told to do in the dream. Not only did he continue with his plans to take Mary as his wife, but he also took on the job of raising and protecting the Son of God. He was one very brave, very faith-filled man.

Chapter 5

Mary
A Baby, Who, Me?
Luke 1:26-38

Just three years ago, I was still a young girl on the verge of becoming a woman. Soon, I would marry my fiancé, Joseph. I had been promised to Joseph as a little girl, as was our custom, and knew all of my life that I would marry him. I loved Joseph as a child and I love him as a young woman, so I was happy to marry him. He is a good man, a carpenter by trade, and would be a good provider. First, he worships God, and second, most importantly, he loves me.

Suddenly, my life became a miraculous whirlwind. I was alone at home one day when this beautiful, terrifying vision appeared in front of me. I wanted to hide and to stare forever, all at the same time. Then the vision spoke. It said, "Hail, thou art highly favored, the Lord is with thee: blessed are thou among women" (Luke 1:28 KJV).

"Whatever did this vision, an angel of God, mean by this saying?" was what passed through my mind. Now I was not only in awe but also confused.

Then the angel said, "Fear not Mary: ('too late for that,' I thought) for thou hast found favor with God, and, behold, thou shalt conceive in thy womb, and bring forth a son, and shalt call his name Jesus. He shall be great and shall be called the Son of the Highest; and the Lord God shall give unto him the throne of his father David; and he shall reign over the house of Jacob forever; and of his kingdom there shall be no end" (Luke 1:30-33 KJV).

Somehow, I found my voice and asked the angel how that could possibly happen since I had never been with a man. It made no sense at all to me, being a virgin.

The angel said that it would happen by the power of the

Highest, so the child to be born of me would be called the Son of God.

Next, the angel told me about another miracle that had already taken place. My cousin Elizabeth, who had been barren and was way beyond childbearing years, was already six months pregnant. I believe it was a sign from God that this was a true vision.

The angel said, "For with God nothing shall be impossible" (Luke 1:37 KJV).

How could I argue with that? So I replied to him, "Behold the handmaid of the Lord, be it unto me according to thy word" (Luke 1:38 KJV).

Ponder—Read Luke 1:2-56

- Mary was a young girl when God chose her. Do you think a young girl today would be as quick to respond affirmatively to God's calling? Would you?

- Mary recognized the angel and found it terrifyingly beautiful. Have you ever had such an experience or an experience when you wanted to stay and go at the same time? What did you do?

My Conclusions

Mary, oh Mary! She was the youngest to share her story here and yet played the greatest part—if you don't count the baby she was carrying, of course. Imagine being a very young woman, on the verge of the coming of age to be married, and then having your whole life turned upside down by an angel who tells you that you are the most blessed of all women. That sure was a lot to live up to. Then she is told that she is to carry and give birth to the Son of God. How very scared and excited she must have been! Every young Hebrew woman wondered if she would be the one to bear the Hebrew people's prophetic king, but none expected it to be her. Then suddenly, Mary was the chosen one.

Chapter 6

Zechariah and Elizabeth
At Last

Luke 1:5-25; 40-80; Matt. 3:13-17; 14:3-10

My name is Zechariah, and I am a priest of the line of Abijah. My wife is Elizabeth, a descendant of Aaron. We have a story to tell you.

We have always been faithful in following our God, Yahweh, and keeping all of His commandments. In spite of this, we were never blessed with children and reached old age without that blessing.

One day I was serving in the Temple as a priest before God, having been chosen at that time to be the priest privileged to go into the temple and burn incense before God. It is an honor to be chosen. There are many priests, and most only get to serve once in a lifetime, if at all. I was excited and reverent as I entered the inner sanctuary. As usual, a large crowd of people was outside the temple praying.

While I was going about my duties, an angel suddenly appeared before me. I must admit that I was not startled; I was shaken to my very core. I had never heard of such a thing happening to any other priest, and I was filled with fear.

Then the angel spoke to me and said, "Do not be afraid, Zechariah; your prayer has been heard. Your wife Elizabeth will bear you a son, and you are to call him John. 14 He will be a joy and delight to you, and many will rejoice because of his birth, 15 for he will be great in the sight of the Lord. He is never to take wine or other fermented drink, and he will be filled with the Holy Spirit even before he is born. [16] He will bring back many of the people of Israel to the Lord their God. [17] And he will go on before the Lord, in the spirit and power of Elijah, to turn the hearts of the parents to their children and the disobedient to the wisdom of the righteous—to make ready a people prepared for the Lord" (Luke 1:13-17 NIV).

I was astonished at this pronouncement. Elizabeth was already well beyond childbearing years, and I was not young either, although I should have remembered our history as a people. Sarah was ninety years old when Isaac was born. I should not have doubted, but I did.

"How can I know this will happen," I asked. After all these years it was very difficult for me to believe such a thing could happen. Elizabeth and I had given up all hope of having a child many years ago.

If anything, the angel became taller, grander, more awesome, and stern. I cowered in front of him as he looked down upon me in astonishment and what was quite possibly anger. No one should be brave enough to anger an angel.

He answered me, saying, "I am Gabriel. I stand in the presence of God, and I have been sent to speak to you and to tell you this good news. ²⁰ And now you will be silent and not able to speak until the day this happens, because you did not believe my words, which will come true at their appointed time" (Luke 1:19-20 NIV).

I was still cowered and looking down when the angel disappeared. I have no idea how long the encounter took—moments, hours, or days might have passed in my befuddled mind. But when I exited the inner sanctum, the crowd was still there. I think some were beginning to think that I had been struck down by God and were debating how to pull my body from the place since no one else could enter. There had been priests who died in the inner sanctum in the past, so we developed a procedure to use a long hook to drag out a body. Little did the crowd know that not only had God not struck me dead, but He had also blessed me beyond belief. I was going to be a father, and my beloved Elizabeth was going to be the mother.

When I came outside, I could not tell the gathered crowd what had happened. I could not speak at all, not even a squeak. I signed to them as best as I could, and they realized I had seen a vision inside the temple.

When my time of service at the temple was up, I went home eager to share the news with Elizabeth. She did not understand or believe what I was trying to tell her, and since I could not speak, I had to sign as best I could. Elizabeth could not read, very few women could, and I was reluctant to write it out for anyone else to read to her. This was too private, just for the two of us for a time.

After some time passed, Elizabeth became pregnant. We were both still surprised, even though the angel told us it would happen. Elizabeth kept herself away from people for the first five months. "The Lord has done this for me," she said. "In these days he has shown his favor and taken away my disgrace among the people" (Luke 1:25 NIV).

No one was more surprised than I was, explains Elizabeth, when Zechariah came home from serving in the temple unable to speak. He tried to tell me what had happened through signing, and I recognized that he had had a visitation from God, but I did not understand what he was telling me at first. I thought he was saying that I was going to have a son. I believed I must have misunderstood him.

Then sometime later, I found myself pregnant. I reveled in my pregnancy and kept myself from other people for the first five months. I wanted to enjoy this blessing from God all to myself for a time, and I was very protective of the little one growing inside me. I was an old woman, and I was taking no chances of losing the precious life within me. I should have known that this was God ordained and thus under His protection, and I did, but I still was not going to take any chances.

When I was about six months pregnant, my relative Mary entered my house, and, suddenly, I felt my baby leap with joy in my womb. Next, while filled with the Holy Spirit, I found myself speaking.

I cried out in a loud voice, "Blessed are you among women, and blessed is the child you will bear! 43 But why am I so favored, that the mother of my Lord should come to me? 44 As soon as the sound of your greeting reached my ears, the baby in my womb leaped for joy. 45 Blessed is she who has believed that the Lord would fulfill his promises to her!" (Luke 1:42-45 NIV).

It was an amazing experience. Our unborn children recognized one another and were overjoyed to be in each other's presence.

Then Mary sang a beautiful song of praise. Tears ran down my face. She has a beautiful voice and there was much devotion and praise that rang out from her.

Mary stayed with me for about three months and then left to return home. She was nervous about returning home and facing everyone, especially Joseph. She was worried about how she would tell him about the baby and if he would believe her. I did my best to reassure her that this was in God's hands and that He would take care of it, and I was right. Joseph assured Mary that she and the baby would be loved and they would be a family.

Suddenly, it seemed, it was time for my baby to be born, and Mary went right out of my head. I gave birth to our baby boy with no complications. Oh, he was a beautiful baby! All of our neighbors and nearby relatives came and rejoiced with us. It was a miraculous moment, and all recognized God had blessed us. Before the birth, I had been pitied or looked down upon because I was barren. Now I was seen as blessed, and oh, how I was. I could not bear to lay my son down for the first week. He was so incredible.

When the baby was circumcised on the eighth day, everyone believed we would name our baby Zechariah, after his father. But I said, "No! He is to be called John" (Luke 1:60 NIV).

They said, "There is no one among your relatives who has that name" (Luke 1:61 NIV). So instead of accepting my word, they asked Zechariah what he wanted to name our baby. I was not pleased that they would not take my word. He was my son, the one I had given birth to. Zechariah "asked for a writing tablet, and to everyone's astonishment he wrote, 'His name is John'" (Luke 1:63 NIV).

Immediately Zechariah regained his voice and began praising

God. Everyone there that day and all who heard the story were fearful and wondered what the child would grow up to be since the Lord's hand was obviously on him. Zechariah prophesied about our son, saying that he would be called the prophet of the Most High, who would go before the Lord to prepare His way and give people knowledge of salvation through repentance and forgiveness of their sins. He spoke much concerning John. It was an amazing prophecy, but I was not surprised that God had much in store for our John, for his was a miraculous birth, and his cousin was also God's miracle.

It was scary thinking about John being a prophet. Most prophets had not been revered or treated well during their lives. It was only after their death that most were recognized and their words preserved. Their lives were difficult, demanding, and totally given over to the service of Yahweh. Yet, I knew from the beginning that God had a special plan and purpose for my John. I suspected that somehow he and Mary's child were tied together. Oh, how right I was.

Our boy continued to grow and became very strong in the spirit of the Most High God. He lived in the wilderness until he was revealed to Israel and began his ministry. He drew people to him, as he was filled with the Holy Spirit, and many people repented and turned back to the Lord.

Then one day, his cousin came to be baptized. John tried to

refuse as he recognized that Jesus was his Lord, but Jesus bade John perform his baptism. As Jesus was coming up from the water, "the Holy Spirit descended on him in bodily form like a dove. And a voice came from heaven: 'You are my Son, whom I love; with you I am well pleased' " (Luke 3:22 NIV).

From that time on, John began pointing people to Jesus, and John's ministry began to grow smaller. He was then taken prisoner for speaking out against the marriage of the current ruler, Herod Antipas, who divorced his wife to marry his sister-in-law, Herodias. Eventually, the ruler was tricked into beheading my John. By that time, Zechariah and I were already in heaven awaiting our beloved son, and we welcomed him home with open arms. John fulfilled all the prophecies concerning him and was indeed "a good and faithful servant."

Ponder—Read Luke 1:5-80; Luke 3:20; Matthew 14:1-1

- Do you think that Zechariah and Elizabeth suffered in lacking a child?

- Have you ever known someone desperate to have a child but is not blessed with one?

- Do you think it is a disgrace for a woman to be barren or that she is cursed by God?

- Why would Zechariah have doubted the angel's words?

- How do you think the angel felt?

- How hard do you think it must have been for Zechariah, a priest of his people, to be unable to speak for almost a year?

- How do you think he and Elizabeth communicated?

- Why do you think Elizabeth hid from the public for the first five months of her pregnancy?

- What do you think people thought when they found out she, a very old woman, was pregnant?

- How did the babies recognize each other? Is that possible?

- Considering this story, what do you think about babies in the womb feeling, hearing, and knowing things months before birth? Is it possible?

- How do you think Elizabeth and Zechariah felt about his Spirit-driven prophecy for their son, John?

- Do you think we will be reunited with loved ones when we reach heaven?

My Conclusions

Zechariah and Elizabeth were faithful Hebrews. They had kept the law and commandments of God their entire lives and worshipped him with reverence. Yet, they must have wondered why they were not blessed with at least one child in their faithfulness. Is it any wonder that Zechariah doubted what the angel Gabriel told him. I don't think he really doubted him so much as it was just impossible for him to believe it! I can only imagine how Elizabeth, who had felt disgraced all those years, must have laughed, cried, and given thanks to God during her pregnancy. I believe it was a treasure she wanted to hold onto just a little while all to herself before she let in the world. Zechariah and Elizabeth would have loved their son unconditionally. More than likely, they worried about the prophecy concerning their baby, and yet, they knew he was special — a promise of God. I feel that by the time John began his actual ministry, both parents had more than likely already proceeded him to heaven and gladly and proudly received him there.

Chapter 7

Mary
Blessed Above All Women

Luke 1:39-56; 2:4-7; 16-19; Matt. 2:1-15

S hortly after the visit from the angel, I hurried to see Elizabeth. I found her just as the angel had said, quite pregnant. When I greeted Elizabeth, it was as if our babies recognized one another from our wombs. Elizabeth greeted me as "the mother of her Lord" because she said her baby leapt in her womb when I spoke. Her baby was to be named John, she said. It was amazing that the two cousins knew each other even from the womb. I wondered what kind of relationship they would grow up to have.

Elizabeth and I had a great visit, but then it was time for me to return home. I would have to face Joseph. How was I going to explain this baby to him? Would he believe me? Would he put me to public shame? Would he refuse to marry me or condemn me as a harlot? I knew he loved me, but he was a man, a proud man. I was scared for myself and, most especially, for my unborn child.

What a surprise when Joseph came for me! He already knew about my pregnancy. An angel had visited him in a dream. He still cared for me and intended to go through with the marriage

A short time later, Joseph put me on my little donkey, and we headed to Bethlehem to register for the census that had been required. Joseph did not want to leave me behind because he feared that I might be ridiculed and judged by others. He was already thinking of my baby, our baby, and me and how he might best protect us. Joseph really is an amazing man.

As we approached Bethlehem, I realized that the baby was almost ready to make its appearance in the world, but I certainly was not ready sitting on the back of a donkey. When Joseph saw I was in distress, we walked faster and faster. Poor little donkey.

Finally, we got to Bethlehem, but to our dismay could find nowhere to stay. The town was overflowing with all the people who had come to register for the census. We got to the very last inn, where the innkeeper met us outside, shaking his head from side to side.

Joseph asked him for a place to stay anyway. We were running out of time. I smiled at the innkeeper and then winced in pain with the contractions that were getting closer. Both the innkeeper and Joseph turned pale. Why were they pale? I was the one having a baby.

The innkeeper offered his stable, and Joseph started to turn him down, but I grabbed his arm and told him it would be ok because we needed a place NOW!

So the innkeeper led us to the little stable, which was clean and warm and had a water supply nearby. I was happy to be off the donkey and able to lie down as the contractions came closer and closer.

Sometime later, I was holding our beautiful baby boy. Joseph washed him, and I wrapped him tightly in strips of cloth and put him in a clean manger to sleep.

Later, as I was resting, there was a commotion, and a group of shepherds pushed the stable door open. They told us they had come to see the newborn Savior of the world that an angel had told them about. They stared at the baby in awe for a time. I smiled at them and inwardly praised God for another sign from him that this little boy was indeed the Son of God.

In keeping with our religious traditions, when the baby was eight days old, he was circumcised, and we named him Jesus. I hated to hear his cries, but of course, Jesus was just fine. At forty days, we presented Jesus at the temple and offered sacrifices in thanks for his birth.

Then we settled down in a little house in Bethlehem for the next two years. It was a time of peace and joy as we watched our little boy grow. Then one night, there was a knock at our door. Three strange men stood there. They told us they were Magi, wise men from the East, who had come searching for the King of the Jews. Theirs had been a long journey, and they had followed a star that led them to us. And yes, when I looked out, there was a big, beautiful star right over our house like a beacon of love. If one knew what to look for, God's signs were everywhere.

The Magi visited with us for a while, worshipping Jesus, who was a toddler by then. They presented some very special gifts to Jesus, which were fit for a king. I smiled at another sign from God that Jesus truly was special, the Son of God.

After the Magi left, Joseph had another dream. He was warned that King Herod would to try to kill our baby. So he woke us up, and we packed up using that same little donkey and snuck out of town in the middle of the night. I was sad that we did not get to say goodbye to the innkeeper who had befriended us, but it was safer for him and us to leave that way.

We arrived in Egypt and settled in to wait until it was safe to return to Israel. At first, it was very hard for me. Joseph was the only one I knew, and the Egyptian culture was very different from our own. But I soon made some friends; Joseph found work with his carpentry skills, and Jesus loved playing with the children there. So there we stayed until we were called back to Israel, and honestly it was not so bad, but I did miss my family and home.

Yes, I was surprised, scared, and amazed at all of the drama surrounding one little boy, but I also kept the memory of each thing in my heart, for I know what a special child he is. One day he will save the world, but right now, he is our little boy crying because he is tired and needs a nap. I will continue to be the best wife and mother I can be and let God take care of the rest.

Ponder—Read Luke 1:2-56

- Why was Mary afraid to face Joseph with her news?

- God had prepared Joseph, just as he had Mary. Do you believe that God has a plan for us, and does He lead us in the way we need to go?

- Did Joseph or Mary have a choice? Why or why not?

- Do you believe that Jesus was an ordinary little boy growing up? Why or why not?

My Conclusions

Then suddenly, Mary was the chosen one. But who would believe her? So, God gave her Elizabeth, her cousin, who was also miraculously pregnant, to recognize who the child Mary was carrying really was. Next, God blessed Mary by revealing to Joseph that Mary was still to be his wife and whose child she was actually carrying. Joseph must have been a great comfort to Mary, whose whole life took on an entirely different and sometimes painful course than she had expected. Was Mary the most blessed of all women? That is a question she must have had from time to time, but I believe that her complete and unconditional love for Jesus would make her answer yes each time.

Chapter 8

ARI, THE LION
HEROD'S CAPTAIN OF THE GUARD

Matthew 2:16-18

My name was Ari, meaning lion, and I did my best to live up to my name as Herod's captain of his guards. I was one of the "Doryphoroi," a part of the Jewish nobility who served as part of Herod's troops.[2] We were absolutely loyal to King Herod.

Herod was a great king in many ways. He enlarged the temple in Jerusalem, built fortifications like Masada, and did many other things to make Judea a country that the Romans would consider important enough to continue keeping us safe.

However, he was also paranoid about his kingdom and remaining king and was bloodthirsty in assuring that he could continue his reign. He had many people killed, including some of his own family members, and I had no qualms carrying out his execution orders. It was my job, and I was good at it. I had been well trained to guard and kill on command. I was the Lion of Herod, and people were often as afraid of me as they were of Herod. I had risen through the ranks until I was

---

[2] "The Army of Herod the Great 39 BCE-4 BCE: Roman Army, Jewish Troops." *Only Pysics.Org,* OnlyPhysics, 2021, onlyphysics.org/the-army-of-herod-the-great-39-bce-4-bce-roman-army-jewish-troops/.

Herod's number one guard, and I was proud of it.

This all changed with one experience, one command. It started with the visit of three Magi. They came asking where the new King of the Jews was to be born. This caused Herod to become paranoid and fearful, and he reacted out of that fear. He was not about to let anyone else become king. He sent the three Magi on their way to Bethlehem to seek the baby with the request that they return and tell him how to find the child so that he also could go and worship him.

As more and more time passed and the Magi did not return, Herod became increasingly impatient and angry. Finally, when he realized they were not coming back, he gave the command that changed everything for me.

He ordered me to take my soldiers, go to Bethlehem and its surrounding areas, and kill each boy child from newborn to two years of age. I tried to reason with him, After all, what harm could a child born in an obscure place like Bethlehem do to a king like Herod? Herod could not hear reason. He commanded me to go, so I took my troops and headed to Bethlehem. I had no qualms when I left to follow those orders. What was one more killing, one more death among the many that I had already committed? I also knew that if I did not go, I would risk losing my place among Herod's elites and could even become a target for his revenge. Neither of those options was very appealing.

My troops and I arrived in Bethlehem, and the slaughter began. We went from home to home, forcing our way in. If we found a boy child who looked anything like a two-year-old or younger, we ran him through with our swords. At first, it was just routine killing for which we were well-trained.

Then those mothers grabbed up their sons, pleaded for their lives, or tried to run from us. We started plunging our swords into the mothers and through those little boys. No one escaped from us. As I looked into the eyes of one mother, I saw her fear, desperation, and humanity. I had never really looked into the eyes to see the soul of one of my victims before, and now I will never be able to forget that look of love, determination, and willingness to die defending her child. She did die, just like so many other mothers trying to save their children. They died together.

By the time the killing was over, Bethlehem was covered in blood, as were my soldiers and I. Instead of the joking and camaraderie my troops usually had after a battle, there was total silence. We all headed to a nearby river, stripped off our war gear, and washed the blood off our swords, spears, and ourselves. By the time we were finished, the water had turned red from the blood, and I swear to this day, I can sometimes still smell the blood on myself.

As we headed back to Jerusalem, a few soldiers tried to speak, joke, lighten up the mood, but all fell silent again after a few tries. I released my troops to go home and rest. I seriously doubt that any of them ever really rested again. I know my memories haunt my sleep, and I pale each time I hear a baby cry.

I returned to Herod to tell him that his orders had been carried out.

He gleefully thanked me. "Wonderful!" he said. "Now I know that the kingdom is safe once again. Thank you, my friend, for looking after me so well."

I had no words for that greeting. I just stared at Herod until he started to squirm under my gaze. He released me to go and get a well-earned rest.

Herod must have sensed that my feelings toward him had changed. I was called less and less into his presence to guard him, and soon he replaced me as his captain and personal guard.

I was grateful to have been released from that position. I hated Herod for what he had commanded me to do, and I hated myself even more for following his command.

I retired from the army. I changed my name from Ari,

meaning lion. I was no longer proud to be a lion, a man-killer. My new name is Shulum, meaning a man of peace. I left my aristocratic family and sought out ways to help people less fortunate.

Those acts by no means bring me peace or forgiveness. I cannot forgive myself, and I honestly cannot believe that God could forgive me either. No amount of sacrifices or good works will ever make up for what I have done.

Occasionally, I run upon a member of my old troops. Several have turned to alcohol or drugs. I heard about the suspicious deaths of a few. Most continue in their role as soldiers, although few have risen up in the ranks as they had been destined to do. That one night took its toll on each of us in different ways.

Many years have passed since that night, and I still seek atonement and peace. I have heard of a man who claims to forgive sins. How can he do that? Only God can forgive sins. Funny thing is, he would be about the same age as those babies we killed if they had lived. Is it possible that God pulled one over on old Herod? I surely hope so. Maybe I will try to find that man, the man called Jesus, and see if he can help me find peace. I doubt it, but who knows?

Ponder—Read Matthew 2:1-9; 12-13; 17-18

- What is the role of a soldier?

- Does a soldier have a choice if he disagrees with a command he is given? Why or why not?

- Would there be consequences for refusing a direct order? What might those consequences be?

- Do you think soldiers ever feel guilty about carrying out some of their orders? Why or why not?

- Have you ever been told to do something that you thought was wrong? What did you do? If you did it, how did you feel afterward?

- Do you know of a soldier, or anyone else, who might be suffering from Post-Traumatic Stress Disorder?

- Can you be excused for doing something you believe is wrong because you were ordered to do it?

- Who bears the blame, the one issuing the order or carrying it out? Why?

- This soldier was looking for peace and forgiveness. Do you think that he could ever find it after what he did? Why or why not?

- Do you need forgiveness for something? Where can you find it?

My Conclusions

The Captain of Herod's Guard was a true soldier. He was trained to follow orders and to kill on command. He was proud of his name, which meant lion, when he was a soldier. He actually seemed to admire Herod and stated that he had no problems carrying out any of Herod's execution orders. Then something happened. He saw the humanity of his victims. He let himself see their fear, their grief, and their willingness to die to protect their children, and he could not live with himself as he was any longer. He changes his name from lion to a man of peace and gives up his life as a killer to help others. Yet, he does not find peace and forgiveness through good works as he had hoped. He is left searching for those things, but there is a moment of hope when he decides to seek out Jesus. The soldier had been a lion, but in the end, he became more of a lamb.

Chapter 9

The Old Shepherd
and
The Good Shepherd

Luke 24; Matt. 28; John 20

The old shepherd continued speaking to his grandsons. "Earlier this week, I saw that baby again, right here in Jerusalem. Of course, he was no longer a baby, but my spirit knew him the minute I saw him. He was teaching in the temple. Many people were amazed at his teachings, but the Pharisees were angry, very, very angry."

"You see, that baby became Jesus of Nazareth. You have all heard of him, his teachings, and his healings. Surely his knowledge and power could only have come from God."

The grandsons were quiet. They all knew about this Jesus of Nazareth and knew that he had been crucified. Now they were beginning to understand the old shepherd's grief. If he really believed that blessed baby and Jesus of Nazareth were the same, how sad he would be.

"But grandfather," one of the grandsons finally spoke up. "How can you be sure that the baby in Bethlehem and this Jesus of Nazareth are the same? Would God truly let the Savior, who was to bring joy to all men, be killed in such a way?"

"I cannot answer that last question my son, but yes, I am sure with all my heart that the baby and Jesus of Nazareth are the same person. You see, my faith has been very strong over the years and it has grown stronger. I do not yet understand God's purpose, but I believe that he has one and that Jesus is the Savior promised by God so many years ago."

Suddenly, one of the other grandsons, who had not gone out to the fields with them, ran up to the group.

"You will not believe what is happening in Jerusalem," he said.

"What is it?" They all asked, fearing another riot or an attack by their Roman conquerors.

"The body of that Jesus of Nazareth who was crucified has disappeared from the tomb. No one could have gotten into that tomb, and yet it is gone. And now there are reports that he has been sighted walking, talking, and even eating with people. Is it possible? Could God have truly brought him back to life?"

They all turned and stared at the old shepherd. He was standing, with his hands lifted toward heaven and praising God. His face glowed with happiness and something else.

He turned to his grandsons and said, "Now we see the plan of God unfolding before us. Jesus said that His Father, God, sent him into the world to save it. And that is just what he has done."

He looked up to heaven and said, "Yes, God has raised him from the dead and he has conquered death. He is the savior that God promised. Just like that unexpected night when God had his angels appear to a lowly group of shepherds, He has done the unexpected to provide his Savior to the world."

"Believe in Him, my sons and grandsons, and put your faith in Jesus. He will change and save the world that believes in Him. Did you know that Jesus said of himself that he is the Good Shepherd? He said that he would know his flock and call them by name, and the flock would come when they heard his voice. He is one of us, and yet He is our Good Shepherd."

The grandsons loved their grandfather and knew he would only speak truth to them. That very night they learned that they had their very own Good Shepherd and that he would never leave nor forsake them. They all put their trust in Jesus and shared this story from generation to generation to all who would hear.

Ponder—Read about the resurrection of Jesus

- The old shepherd appeared to have a divine revelation from God the night the angels appeared to him, which changed his life. Do you think there is such a thing as a divine revelation today? How would it change a person?

- Do you believe that a revelation could strengthen your belief in something?

- The grandsons did not see the angels, yet they followed the belief of their grandfather. Why would his grandsons believe him?

- Do you have any family traditions or beliefs that have been passed down that your family treasures as truth? Can you share them?

- How do you think the old shepherd knew that the Jesus he saw in the temple was the same baby he worshipped thirty-three years earlier?

- Why do you think that Jesus called himself the good shepherd?

- What would make a good shepherd? Find in the Bible where Jesus tells what a good shepherd is and describe it here.

- Do you need a good shepherd? Why or Why not?

My Conclusions

The last short story has the old shepherd recognizing that Jesus is the Good Shepherd who takes care of his lambs. He beseeches his grandsons to believe in and follow Jesus, the Good Shepherd, and they do because of their grandfather's testimony.

Final Conclusion

Each of the people in these stories saw the birth of the baby Jesus through their own eyes and experiences. And each story was different, special to each person. Yet, each person also had some questions and some decisions to make.

And you, what do you think about that baby boy? What do your eyes see in him? Just like each of these, you have a choice to make. It is yours and yours alone. And the story of your choice is only yours to tell.

Part II

"O Come Let Us Adore Him
The Companion Stories

These animal stories come purely from my imagination. My original intention was to write them for children, but along the way, I discovered I am not a children's writer—not yet anyway. I pray that you consider this a bit of fun and "what ifs" about the animal and heavenly kingdom.

Psalms 66:4 teaches us that, "All the earth shall worship thee, and shall sing unto thee; they shall sing *to* thy name" (NIV). The animals in the stories reveal that, as inhabitants of Earth, they also praise and serve our Father, Abba, and our Risen Savior, Jesus. I hope you enjoy the telling of their tales.

Billie Stultz

Chapter 1

Dutimus
The Great Brouhaha

*Dutimus means having great character
and the power for miracles and making war.*

D utimus[3] watched over his flock from his sentry point between the flock and the shepherds. The shepherds also watched while at their campfire telling stories of their great adventures from years past. It was a quiet evening, and he had his best sentries, led by his second-in-command named Liam, in position at good distances to keep a watch over all. Dutimus was looking forward to a quiet night and some well-deserved rest for him and his small band of sheep herding dogs.

The flock was also well trained. Dutimus would accept no less when he was in charge. Every sheep, including the lambs, would turn in unison to face Dutimus and await his instructions at a certain stance or bark of the dogs. It was a good life but not a life anyone would have expected from his rough beginnings with the herd. The grandfather shepherd found him several seasons back as he wandered a bit too close to that flock in search of food. The young Dutimus had been in the caravan of a king traveling through to a distant land and somehow became separated from his master. Lonely and

---

[3] Dutimus adapted from *dunamis*. See: Griffin, Annette. "What Is Dunamis, and What Kind of Power Does Jesus Give Believers?" *Bible Study Tools,* 2022, www.biblestudytools.com/bible-study/topical-studies/what-is-dunamis-and-what-kind-of-power-does-jesus-give-believers.html.

afraid, the shepherd's kind eyes lured him in that night, and Dutimus had been with him ever since.

The shepherd came to love Dutimus and trained him to become, quite possibly, the best sheep-working dog in the entire world. The night of the great brouhaha, as Dutimus called it, became almost too much for even him to manage.

It started with the brightest night sky Dutimus had ever seen. It was that one point of light, a star the shepherd called it. The sky was so well lit that he would not need to worry about any predatory animals sneaking into the flock. He felt his eyes getting heavy after he turned the reigns over to Liam, and then he heard it begin. It was a brouhaha that began with sounds from the sky. It was not the normal booming sounds that came with rain showers or the sound of birds swooping over, but a sweet and thunderous sound, something like the little shepherds when they stroked the box of strings or put the river reed to their mouth. Only this sound filled the whole sky, and it was beautiful. Every sheep turned in unison to face the things made of light that hung in the sky. He decided they were new birds, with wings holding them in the air and songs coming from them.

All at once the songs stopped, the birds began to move away toward the town, and then, the most surprising thing of all, the shepherds stood, left the fire and followed them. Every single shepherd walked away, from the grandfather down to the littlest grandson. No one remained to help him watch the flock. "Goodness," he snorted. "What is this about?" No matter, he had the sheep back when the strange birds turned away. All sheep were looking toward him for instructions. Liam was waiting orders as well, and that is when Dutimus noticed that Izzy, the troublemaker, was on the move and gaining on the shepherd's position.

Dutimus stamped his paw and let out a series of barks and a howl. Izzy had been recently trained to know that howl meant stopping in his tracks and looking around until he spotted Dutimus for an order to get him out of some new predicament. However, Izzy took no notice of him and bounced behind the shepherds. Dutimus let out a low growl, determined to let Izzy go this time and suffer the consequences of his choice. As he turned back to the flock to take stock of the situation, he caught sight of Izzy's mother. She was the matriarch of the flock and thus garnered a great deal of respect from the dogs. She bleated a plea. With a deep sigh, Dutimus barked control of the ninety-nine to Liam and turned to start after that one. This would not be an Izzy moment when he caught up with him. This moment would be a full-out Israel, Izzy's full name, moment. His given name became Israel when he wandered off from his mother as soon as he could walk, seeking only God knows what adventure.

Dutimus found it difficult to keep his focus on the little lamb as he was captivated by the glowing light in the night sky that the shepherds were now following. He followed the procession right into town, a place he had not been since he lost his way long ago. He had become faithful to grandfather shepherd and never left his side unless it was to take up position with the flock. He bumped into Izzy, not realizing the group stopped outside a stable. Before he could latch onto Izzy, that little adventurer slipped in between all the shepherds and right into the stable. Dutimus did not like this at all. Who could know what kind of danger awaited them in that place? He preferred open spaces where he could easily spot approaching trouble.

He followed grandfather shepherd in and quickly realized there was no danger here. There was only a soft, pretty female shepherd and a tired, but kind-looking male. He was able to advance to a feeding trough and snatched Izzy out of a mid-air bounce as Izzy was planning to get some food without being invited. As Izzy swung back and forth in Dutimus' mouth, Dutimus looked into the trough and saw the tiniest little shepherd he had ever seen. "Is this how shepherds started out," he wondered? No matter, he must deal with Izzy. As he started to back away, the tiny one made the sound of shepherds' joy, a laugh they called it, reached its little hand to pat Izzy, and then reached for Dutimus' long muzzle. Dutimus had never been so drawn to any shepherd or animal, not even grandfather or his best buddy, Liam. Izzy bounced off the floor as Dutimus released him, stepped up, lowered his face close to the little one, sniffed and gently kissed the tiny hand. Dutimus and the tiny shepherd looked thoughtfully into each other's eyes. Grandfather, the other shepherds, and even Izzy turned to go. Dutimus took one step back, but could not bear to move away from his new, new what? The word master rose up from within him, and he knew that this was his place, but what about grandfather shepherd? Grandfather seemed to understand as he knelt slowly beside Dutimus and looked into the crib with him. He stroked Dutimus carefully, looked at the female and male in the stable, and they all smiled and nodded. "Dutimus, my faithful companion," he said, "you have a new lamb to watch over now. You must stay here, with this family. The little one will become your master when he is able. Until then, yield to his parents for instructions." He rose and then added, "Liam is ready. He will faithfully serve me now. I will miss you, old friend." With one more stroke of Dutimus' head and back, grandfather was gone. Dutimus settled in next to the trough and laid his head on his paws with a clear view of the only entrance in case any others might approach. He had a new master and a new home, wherever they took him.

Chapter 2

Sozo's Tale
Delivered to Delivery

Sozo means saved, healed and delivered.

She is resting, finally. My person, Mary, is sleeping slightly, her new little person sleeping in a trough by her side. Her man, Joseph, is standing between them and the stable door. He is reading the stars. I did not know about him at first, but he is guarding her well, and I can see that she does not want to be without him.

I can rest a bit after our long journey. My eyes drift and close, and I dream of days long gone.

My birth was quite an event for the young Nazarene family. They were happy and thanking their Hebrew God that my mother was adding a foal to the family. My family line is graced with gifted and extraordinary donkeys. Balaam's donkey is just one of my distant relatives who have a place in donkey and human history.

On my birth night, my brother was born first, and they all gathered to admire him as he struggled to stand. Mother worked to clean him, and then the unexpected and amazing took place. I came along. Mother paused her attention to brother, lay on her side and brayed long and loud as I struggled to emerge into the night of the new moon. I brayed as I entered the world but could not stand as one of my back legs was turned. No matter how hard I tried, I could not lift myself on three good legs. Everyone, even mother and brother, looked at me with sadness and then looked to the family papa to see his decree. He looked down, slowly shook his head, patted my mother to comfort her and then bent down to scoop me up. He would carry me away to handle the lame foal in the accepted way, but, miraculously, I was saved by a most beautiful human person I saw for the first time that night.

My person, Mary, stepped into her papa's way, gently touched his forearm, and said, "Wait, papa. I can take him. I can help him. Please, papa. Let me try to save him." Later, I learned that Mary had never asked her papa for anything. She was a good, obedient, respectful daughter. She never questioned her papa but did as she knew he would want her to do. But this night, she stopped him from his course of action, and I was saved.

She got up early, stayed awake late to finish her chores, and still spent time with me. Every day she massaged my lame leg with a poultice she made from every herb she could find in nearby fields and forests. She spoke kindly to me, telling me I was special and would have extraordinary work to do one day. She spoke healing from her God over me. As I grew stronger under her care, I did stand one day; next, I walked, and finally, I could go to the fields with my brother to work the sheep. My specialty was catching the scent of any approaching coyotes or wild dogs. I could stare them down and frighten them away from our herd with my eyes alone.

My mother also began to tell me I was special. She said I would be given important tasks that only I could accomplish. I took my place in the donkey family and grew stronger day by day. And my person, Mary, made sure she stopped by the stable at least once daily to rub my ears and praise my progress. She became my best friend.

When she left her papa's house to make her own home with her man called Joseph, her papa made her a gift of me. He told her that he knew he could not separate us. He told Joseph that he must procure at least one more donkey because donkeys need family around us to thrive, and Joseph agreed. But I brayed and brayed, trying to make him understand Mary is my family.

To begin our new life, Mary led me to a tiny stable, big enough for only me, next to her and Joseph's tiny home. And I was just fine. Then, to my surprise, late one evening, Joseph and Mary talked excitedly about making a trip, a long journey. Mary said she could not go without me, but Joseph did not believe I was strong enough to make the journey. Not to be left behind if Mary needed me, I busted out the wall of my stable and marched right into their presence, braying every step of the way. Lanterns were lit up and down our tiny street to see what was causing the ruckus. Joseph threw his head back and laughed. He then threw his hands into the air in surrender. Mary and I had our way; that is how I became the donkey with the very special task of carrying my person Mary and her babe, who they named Jesus, through the night to his birthing.

As I enjoyed the peace of my delightful reverie of memories, another ruckus broke out to wake me. This time, my ears perked up and then flattened in my extreme, threatening signal. Joseph admitted a herd of shepherds, an annoying, tiny lamb who bounced all over the stable, and then the final insult, a dog. I began to bray my warning. Joseph, what have you done? No dog can come near sheep or my people. I began to bray louder, stare, and slowly advance on the interloper. Ignoring me, the dog advanced on the lamb, clutching it by its neck in a mid-air jump.

I knew I had to find a way to deal with him. I may not appreciate this lamb's erratic behavior, but that did not make it alright to watch him killed so brutally. I lined up to deliver a rib-crushing kick, people moved quickly to separate us animals and then everything stopped instantly. Baby Jesus made a noise. A tiny, little bray of joy. Baby Jesus reached for the lamb swinging from the slobbery dog's mouth, patted the lamb, and then, to my absolute astonishment, Jesus patted the dog. The dog dropped the lamb and nuzzled our baby. That dog then looked at each of us with a clear challenge should we try to stop him and settled himself next to the trough as if taking up guard. His eyes settled on mine, and we held a stare. After looking between the two of us to be sure neither was moving in aggression, the dog's old shepherd person spoke to Joseph. The shepherd then patted the dog and said something to him. The dog smiled at him, and the shepherds and the lamb left. That dog did not move.

Without breaking my stare, I stepped toward him to kick him out, but Mary looked at him and then me and said, "Sozo[4], meet Dutimus. He is your family now."

I delivered my person here to give birth to her child after she saved and claimed healing for me. How could I deny her anything? But a dog? She simply smiled and reached out to stroke my ears. Fine, but he's not sleeping in my stable.

---

[4] "Sozo." *Bible Study Tools*, 2022,
www.biblestudytools.com/lexicons/greek/nas/sozo.html.

Bemacheval
The Dance of Praise

*Bemacheval means to dance, spin
and twirl before the Lord in praise.*

B emacheval[5] glided slowly and smoothly into the river. The cool waters washed over his body, and he smiled a smile of pure refreshment as he gently spun in a semi-circle before reversing and dipping his whole head into the waters while performing a graceful underwater bow no one would be able to see and appreciate. He felt the ripples of current wash over him before he began to drink in what he would need to sustain him for the long journey ahead. He had been awakened from dreaming of a slow, flowing dance in a rhythm to match a gentle rain on a breezy day he had felt only a very few times in his life. Most days, he danced into the waters, kicking up droplets over all of his herd. "Bemacheval," the camel mothers would shout, "you are about to drown the babies. Stop that prancing." But the entire herd knew even the mothers turned from him and half smiled, enjoying his joyful spirit. It was hard for a camel or man to be near Bema and not catch the presence of delight in the entire journey of life he almost always carried.

There was one, however, who could not be bothered with what he, an amazingly wise man, saw as Bemacheval's foolishness.

---

5 "HEBREW WORD STUDY – DANCING." *Chaimbentorah.com,* WordPress.org, 2022, www.chaimbentorah.com/2020/02/hebrew-word-study-dancing/.

Wise One One, number one, as the herd thought of him, could read the stars, predict the future and discern men's goodness or evil. Still, he did not appreciate Bema's zeal for daily routine tasks or for the more extraordinary adventures the group undertook from time to time. The upcoming trip was no exception for either Bema or number one. Bema vibrated with bubbling energy.

The camel herd came up out of the water. Most camels stomped, shook, and allowed the water to drain from them as the camel drivers came to load and organize them into a train for the start of the trip. Bemacheval was in rare form as his gliding waltz-like swim turned into a jazz tap, complete with his sweeping sand every which way. When he made it into his assigned place in line, near the front, he noticed that what followed him was a path with a series of lines and dips and curves in the sand. It resembled the ink scratching the wise ones made on parchment in the evenings around the campfires. He looked back, admiring his ability to mimic their scratchings, and nearly ran into Wise One Two and Three who were deep in conversation about which camel should be where in the line. Bema quickly stood at attention, not wanting to start the trip suffering under their displeasure.

Wise One Two and Three's discussion ended with quiet laughter as they signaled the driver and gave orders for the arrangement of camels, and Bemacheval found himself very near the front and bearing a riding saddle. He was pleasantly astonished. He was generally given freight to carry at the very end of the train. None of the wise ones wanted to ride him because he often forgot that he was not to dance while carrying wise ones, and they became ill with his motions. Other camels complained of the dust he generally kicked up as he practiced his latest dance creations. He tried to explain that if he could get cooperation from all of them in the herd, he could put on a show the wise ones would watch with rapt attention in the evenings. He was confident that after the show, the Wise Ones would smile, laugh and sleep better for the joy. If only. But he snapped back to the moment and wiggled until the saddle felt right between and around the humps on his strong back. Then he waited to see which Wise One he would have the honor to transport.

Suddenly, his world slammed to a screeching halt as Wise One One stepped up, climbed the steps next to him and sat with a heavy thump atop Bemacheval. Bema cautiously peered over his shoulder. Did One not notice he had just perched himself upon Bema? Bema quickly turned his face away and determined to move as smoothly as possible to win the approval of One, a recognition not only sought by all in the herd but also a tribute no realistic camel ever believed would be granted. And so it began, the drive of the century.

Wise One One turned and looked back at Two and Three. He

knew they were up to something as each smiled self-satisfactorily, but "what were they up to?" was the question. They had lately taken to determining a course of light-hearted disruptions to his typically very ordered daily schedule and life. To what end, he could not determine. Oh, how he despised caravan trips; he had only agreed to venture with this one because One knew, with a certainty he was sometimes blessed with, that this trip would change the world. As he began to complete the turn back to the direction in which he was moving, his eye caught sight of what looked like writing in the sand. Who would have painstakingly written King David's words in the sand? He recognized it as a prophecy of David, perhaps for such a time as this, "A posterity shall serve Him. It will be recounted of the Lord to the next generation. They will come and declare His righteousness to a people who will be born, that He has done this." (Psalms 22:30-31, NKJV). The words faded from his sightline, and he felt a rhythmic, almost massaging, gentle dip and sway as his camel took up his gait in obedience to the drivers.

It was not until the first night that One realized the camel he rode was Bemacheval. As One climbed down and began to pat his approval for the excellent ride on the front haunch of the animal, he recognized Bema. He withdrew his approving hand, grunted, and walked away, catching sight of Two and Three, who were watching and laughing loudly. So this was their scheme, to give him the roughest ride out of all the camels. The wise men had committed their lives to these ships of the sea for the duration of the excursion. His friends jokingly meant for his ride to be rough. But after today's pleasant ride, better than any camel ride he had experienced his entire life, the joke may be on them, he thought; however, he would not give them or Bemacheval the satisfaction of that knowledge. Bema moved to the herd to hear a lecture about not disturbing anyone's rest with his antics, but it was a moot point as he slipped into a deep sleep when he reached them. Working all day to give a smooth, rejuvenating ride to One was exhausting. He had no energy left for dancing this night or for many nights to come.

As the excursion train moved on and on, One noticed that although Bemacheval was supremely focused on his gait and provided the same wondrous ride as that first day, something was missing from Bema. His energy and life force were more and more drained. It seemed to take all he had to put one hoof in front of the other and absorb the movement and heat of the sands. One even became concerned for Bema's wellbeing. He quietly and secretly began giving the camel pats of recognition each evening and even massaged the neck several times. Bema welcomed and accepted the gracious acknowledgments, but it hardly made a difference as he plodded off to rest with the herd each evening. Perhaps, One thought, he had been too harsh with Bemacheval after Dutimus' disappearance. But, no, if the camel had not coaxed his loyal dog to be up every night playing or dancing, as it somehow appeared, Dutimus, his best companion, would never have been lost from the caravan and from One's life. Bemacheval had somehow become a splendid caravan camel, but he could never earn One's true affection.

The train paused just outside a palace and remained there for several evenings. As Bemacheval approached the herd and again fell into an immediate, fitful sleep, the others whispered their concerns for him. What was happening to their friend? He had changed. Was it the pressure of the lead position, or had One extinguished the camel's flame of joy forever? Although Bema was beyond annoying most of the time, he was greatly missed when he was so diminished among them. He was the one who kept them laughing and sighing every evening on these trips. He kept all their hearts pumping with life. They moved around him to be sure he was protected and got rest for the night.

The next day the train moved on to a small village called Bethlehem. The three lead camels were loaded with a few additional items. Bema caught a scent that transported him as close to joy as he had felt in months. The rest of the train remained outside the village, and the three wise ones rode in alone. They made many brief stops as the wise ones inquired about a location until they stopped outside an inn. Bema spotted a small manger structure to the side and knew that neither he nor his companions would fit in there, so it would be another night under the stars. To his surprise, the innkeeper moved quickly in front of them and led the way to another place. The wise ones dismounted and entered the dwelling leaving Bema a moment to rest and mildly investigate these new surroundings. Not that he made any serious effort, just enough to find a suitable place to rest should this be the end of their travel for the evening, and that is when he spotted something dark and small moving toward them rapidly. As he hoped this was not a creature he would need to deal with, it came into focus and something familiar in the trot caught his attention. As it moved closer and closer, Bema could see its fur standing on end and hear a low, menacing growl directed toward him.

As it came close, he was astounded to recognize an old friend. Could it be; yes, it was his soul brother, Dutimus. "Dutimus, Dutimus, my brother," he hollered as he began a trot to meet the long-missing dog. Then, from nowhere, a powerful donkey kick rammed Bema's side, knocking him off balance and into the other two camels, and they all went down, bing, bang, bong. In the mystifying scramble of crisscrossed camel legs, a donkey's relentless kicks, and a dog's excited jumping in and amongst it all, the home's door flew open. Out ran three very confused wise ones and a man named Joseph carrying a small child who was laughing with delight. All commotion stopped as they all turned their gaze on the little boy as if he commanded them to be still. And they were still. Finally, Wise One One, seeing Dutimus, called out, "my friend, where have you been? Is it you after so many years?" The dog jumped into his arms, knocking him to the ground, and covered him in dog kisses as One lay on the ground sputtering and laughing. Bema was up and dancing in celebration at the unexpected reunion. Was this, he wondered, why we took this journey?

Once they all caught their breath, Joseph, the child, and the wise ones followed Dutimus' lead into the home.

Sozo approached Bemacheval and introduced himself as a servant donkey to the family and Dutimus' boon companion.

Bema gave him a playful kick and complimented Sozo on his extraordinary donkey back kick, asking if he had ever considered a dance line. The two moved away in deep conversation about the glorious benefits of a good kick to a dance line. Sozo began to detail the story of Dutimus' adventures with the shepherds, his excellent herd control skills, and how he had become a companion to the family's young lad. Bema was sad Dutimus had not stayed to visit but quickly understood his friend's new loyalty to the little family and knew that in the dwelling was his rightful place.

Once everyone else was safely asleep, Wise One One lovingly visited Dutimus, telling him that he now understood why his faithful dog had been separated and lost from the caravan.

It was apparent that the God of Abraham had another more vital assignment for the dog, and the loyalty Dutimus felt toward the child was well placed. He released Dutimus to stay, and in forgiveness, One let go of his anger toward Bema, who was to become his new companion. Bema and Dutimus did a little dance they had learned long ago. Sozo kicked and brayed his approval and moved off to try the moves himself. The friends all said goodbye as the wise ones mounted their camels and started toward the caravan outside of town. Bema paused and turned so he and One could give a final wave to Dutimus and Sozo as Dutimus returned to the dwelling's doorstep to take up his place for the evening.

Chapter 4

Dutimus and
the Baby Boy, Jesus
The Destiny of a Companion

Dutimus lay next to the pallet of the boy, his boy as Dutimus thought of him. The boy's mother and father called him Jesus. Dutimus was never truly happy unless he was by the side of Jesus. As Jesus lay in the manger trough on the night of his birth and Dutimus took up watch over him, the destiny of Dutimus as the boy's companion was also born that night.

The family soon moved from the stable into a tiny home not far from the inn where Jesus was born. Dutimus was with the family of three every moment. He walked close by the side of the mother, called Mary, who usually carried baby Jesus, and kept an eye out for any signs of danger that could approach from any direction. He and the father, called Joseph, were always on high alert.

As baby Jesus grew over the following years, Dutimus never wanted to leave him unattended. Occasionally, however, usually during the baby's feeding time, Mary insisted Dutimus go out and get some exercise in the fresh air. Because he knew he must remain strong to truly protect the young boy, Dutimus relented and would leave the home for short periods.

On these excursions around Bethlehem, Sozo, the family donkey, usually accompanied him. They were an odd pair, the large black dog and the small donkey.

Dutimus and Sozo greeted everyone they met as they galloped leisurely or sprinted about town on a mission to keep Dutimus in top physical form.

Some days they would help a neighbor woman carry her

clothing to be laundered at the nearby stream or perhaps a mother carrying a water jug and needed a hand corralling a wandering toddler.

During the first year of Jesus' growing up days, Dutimus and Sozo became what could only be described as neighborhood ambassadors.

They greeted and welcomed kind, good people and warned those whom they rightly perceived to be of less than good report to keep moving until they were far away from the home of Jesus, Mary and Joseph. It was a good life, and the five-member family was happy.

There were many moments of laughter and fun in those first few years of family life. However, none retold around the family more than a day before Jesus's first birthday when Jesus pulled up to stand by Dutimus' side for the first time.

Jesus had been playing with Dutimus all morning. He would crawl around his faithful companion, pulling on ears, legs, feet, and even Dutimus' muzzle. There were many times Dutimus was poked playfully in both eyes, but he never complained or moved away from baby Jesus. If Jesus was playing with him, that just meant he was close enough to provide protection if it should be needed.

Mary was washing some breakfast dishes in a basin across the room, and Joseph had been outside finishing a table the Innkeeper had commissioned him to build for the inn. As Joseph came in to call Mary out to see the finished project, he stopped short and yelled, "Mary. MARY! Look at Jesus!"

Mary spun around in panic, dropping a dish and spilling her water basin as her eyes searched the room for baby Jesus. "Where is he?" she shouted to Joseph.

She had only turned her back for a moment, and Dutimus had been lying right by Jesus' side as he always did unless she forced him out of the house for his daily run with Sozo.

And then she spotted him. Jesus was seated squarely in the center of Dutimus' back, holding onto the fur at the base of the dog's neck, riding as if he were atop a black stallion.

The dog and baby Jesus simply looked at Joseph and Mary as if to say, "What's the big deal. We're just having a ride." And as they proceeded toward the door to expand their territory, Joseph jumped into their path, by now roaring with laughter, and told them that a small circle in the home's main room would have to do for now.

Any time someone in the family retold the story, as Joseph did that evening to Unc the Innkeeper, the bareback dog ride seemed to grow more daring and dangerous. Mother Mary would pretend to be upset with Father Joseph for not stopping the practice and forbidding it ever to happen again, but he would say that boys do need to be boys. Then Mary would turn away from them all and smile her little smile as she once again pondered all these things in her heart.

Jesus and Dutimus had many more adventures as Jesus grew into a curious, intelligent boy, a young man, and, finally, a full-grown man. It seemed that in this daily contact with Jesus that Dutimus grew younger and stronger each year instead of succumbing to the normal aging process. Dutimus' black fur became tinted with white a bit more each year, but his energy and focus only grew stronger.

The dog almost never left the boy's side in those growing-up years and even slipped into the temple in Jerusalem one time, but that is a story for telling another time.

When it was time for Jesus to leave the home of his earthly parents and family, he commissioned Dutimus to stay and look after Mary, his mother. He told his faithful companion dog, who was finally beginning to slow down and show a bit more age after all the miraculous years with Jesus, that Mary needed Dutimus more now. She was getting older, and Jesus knew she would miss him terribly as he left to begin his ministry.

Dutimus did as commanded, as he always did. He loved Mary

and saw it as a privilege and honor to watch over the mother of his master. When he was no longer in the daily life-giving, light-filled presence of Jesus, the dog's life settled into a steady rhythm of daily rest and sleep at the feet of Mary until, in his sleep one night, he went home to heaven.

Although until that evening, Dutimus missed Jesus terribly and mainly slept with one eye open hoping his boy would return to his childhood home to greet Dutimus once again. That reunion, however, would wait until later when they were both in heaven and could walk side by side down a new set of streets in their new hometown.

Chapter 5

Naba
A Long-Awaited Assignment

Pronounced naw-bah. Hebrew for to prophesy through song, to overflow with joy or, to the other extreme, to burp out words.

As Gabriel ushered a tiny resident into his new home, Creature Land, he introduced Gideon, the field mouse, as a mighty warrior and a protector of Mary, God's most blessed among women. The formal introduction was made to Naba[6] the angel, the Creature Land gatekeeper and guide to all creatures new to heaven. Gabriel explained to the frightened little mouse that any creature loved by a human or faithful in service to Abba, Father God, would always have an eternal home here in heaven.

"Naba," Gabriel said with a glowing smile, "let us tell Gideon your story of adventure and what you do when you are not here serving as gatekeeper and host to God's beloved creatures." Gabriel paused and added, "And do not belch it forth in your sometimes rambling fashion. Give the story its due telling with song and accompanying dance." Naba smiled as he knew one of Gabriel's favorite pastimes was telling this story. And so he and Gabriel, mostly Gabriel, began the telling.

Gabriel recalled Naba's work on his latest sculpture was almost complete. It was, in his own words, "a grand design" and took up most of the eastern sky over Bethlehem. There were many of Naba's artistic cloud creations, great and small,

---

[6] "Naba`." *Bible Study Tools,* 2022, www.biblestudytools.com/lexicons/ hebrew/kjv/naba-2.html.

playing in the wonderland of blue sky. With his gentle breath, the creatures moved effortlessly from attraction to attraction, where they spun, slid or strolled through the wispy, white sun-drenched canvas. Just as Naba was about to begin work on another section of blue sky, he felt the presence of someone watching his work, watching him.

Naba continued, "In a brief panic, I wondered if I had once again allowed myself to be distracted by my joy in creating my cloud art and had missed an important moment for the one I finally had been assigned to guard, Dutimus. He is a very important dog. Guardian angels have the highly esteemed job of watching over their human charges to be certain that they are able to complete the work the Father has purposed for them. Sometimes it means suggesting a plan of action into the ear of the human, or it may mean finding ways to shift their path to keep them from danger. The angels then report back to heaven about their humans' path. It is a most important job.

Gabriel recollected the day that Naba's excitement in one of his cloud-shaping artistic achievements had trumped his concern about being caught unfocused on Dutimus. Naba turned to seek the face of his watcher, hoping to share the pure joy of creating. And there, towering above him, looking down at him with less than excited appreciation, was none other than his tribal leader of leaders, the one who had granted him his long-held dream of becoming a guardian in the human world, me. I am Gabriel, and I am in command of the tribes of angels assigned as messengers and guardians, among others.

Once he recognized who was watching him, Naba jumped up from his reclining position beside his charge, Dutimus, who was keeping a keen watch over his flock from a hilltop vantage point. At the same time, his angelic guardian moved clouds around in the sky. "Gabriel," Naba stammered, his jubilation dampened by the possibility that he had been too lightly focused on the assignment yet again, "welcome to my wonderland. Do you like the creatures' sky play land over Bethlehem? My charge, Dutimus, has been calmly resting and gazing at the show I have created to promote his relaxation and relief of stress."

"Really?" queried Gabriel. "To me, Dutimus' gaze seems directed down the hillside. Down, in fact, to his own assigned guardianship duties, the flock. Quite an important fellow he is, you know. He is almost regal in his deportment. His steadfast work ethic is a joy to Abba, Father, and part of the reason he, a creature, is assigned a heavenly guardian. My heartfelt desire is that his work ethic be translated to those who come into his sphere of influence," Gabriel said with a firm yet gentle remonstrance. He shook his head and could not wholly repress a sideways smile as he glanced at the nearly completed sculpture that was beginning to drift away with the

Earth's moving airstreams.

"Yes, sir," Naba sighed with a deep breath, "message received. Dutimus will not leave my visual field again. It will not be like the night he became lost in the wilderness, the night he and I danced with the camel and both lost our focus and his way."

"Good," chimed Gabriel, "because his big moment is quickly approaching, and he will need your guidance."

"Oh, my! Yes, Sir! I am on the job, and I will not let Dutimus, you or Abba down," Naba practically shouted, coming to attention complete with a flourish of salute and a kick-ball-chain pirouetting dance step he simply could not stop from bubbling out of his feet. Gabriel understood better than Naba knew that the Father had created the little angel to worship in song and dance. Gabriel also enjoyed Naba's worship through beautifully artistic creations in the clouds within the Father's natural world.

Gabriel clearing his throat to resume the business of the important day sounded like thunder to the nearby shepherds, "We shall see," Gabriel said, "We shall see." And with a sweep of his wings, Gabriel shot through the middle of the cloud sculpture and disappeared.

Naba looked skyward, fluttering his much smaller wings, and sang out, "Holy Spirit. Holy Spirit, Holy Spirit, where are you?

Are you riding on my clouds? Are you sitting on a beam of sunlight? Are you hiding in the trees? I need you now, please. Please? I need you to quicken my focus, to help me keep my thoughts on my charge, Dutimus." Naba looked through the hole Gabriel had split his sculptured cloud-world with and saw Holy Spirit peeking through it. "Ah, there you are, playing in my wonderland. I knew you would like it. So, good. Stay near, please. I shall need your wisdom."

Naba was careful to stay with Dutimus for the remainder of the day. Normally, he would ride astride the dog's broad back and help him direct the sheep to their proper paths. Naba watched carefully all around them because Gabriel had said the big moment was near, and Gabriel always gave his messages at the exact right timing. Naba wished he had earned enough clearance in Gabriel's tribe to know the precise moment ahead of time, but that honor came with many successful missions completed, and he was still on his way to earning his stripes. He never knew why it was so, but he knew deep within himself that he had always been a favorite of Gabriel. The chief of his tribe, the messenger angel of Abba, God Himself, often came to Naba's territory, Creature Land, to walk and talk with the little angel. He listened quietly, patiently, and with a quick smile as Naba laid out plans for the next improvement for the creatures' enjoyment of their land. Gabriel cherished anything that made Abba smile, and Abba loved His animals. All of heaven knew it was so. Had He not, after all, designed the ark to house not only the family of humans who would continue to inhabit and populate the Earth after the flood but also one of each of His creatures? It was not a question to be pondered. It was just so.

And so, after years, centuries, and eons that seemed like an endless time of Naba trying to convince Gabriel to allow him to become a guardian angel in the human realm, Gabriel finally assented and sent him to guard Dutimus, a critical warrior for heaven on Earth. Naba did not know that Dutimus was in the human world but was, in fact, a creature. Naba, for a second, thought about feeling disappointment, but he could not contain his pure joy at being a part of a creature's life before it entered the heavenly realm for its eternal reward. Naba decided to make Gabriel proud.

The day was fairly typical as any day since Naba had come to live with Dutimus. The shepherds were gathered around the evening fire, and Dutimus seemed ready to hand over the flock to his second in command, Liam. That meant that Dutimus would settle into a light sleep, and Naba could keep an eye on him and stargaze. Stars could not be as easily moved as clouds, but there was always a chance to find one willing to chisel off a beam to become a shooting star, and the fireworks show would be in progress.

This night, however, was to be anything but typical. Just as things seemed to settle down a notch on the energy output scale, Naba observed one, then another, and then hundreds, no thousands, of streaks of light in the night sky. He knew these to be the travel patterns of the Host, God's heavenly army. "What," he mused as he jumped to his feet and hovered above the ground in excitement, "could be going on in a field filled with sheep, a few shepherds, and a faithful sheepdog that would attract the attention of the Host?"

The Host appeared in formation above the hillside and began singing the most beautiful worship Naba had ever heard. Even in heaven, he had not heard a song like this. They were singing about the birth of the King, the Word, of Jesus, and Naba was here to listen to it. Unable to hold back the flood of joy, he burst into song and a flurry of dance and joined in the crescendo. He added a tenor and a texture to the music that would have been impossible without him. He bubbled over with pure joy and accented the harmonious sound with the timbre of shooting stars. It became a cacophony of light and sound created at that moment for that moment and as the backdrop to Gabriel's message. The chief messenger said to the shepherds, "Fear not: for behold, I bring you good tidings of great joy, which shall be to all people. For unto you is born this day in the city of David a Saviour, which is Christ the Lord. And this shall be a sign unto you; Ye shall find the babe wrapped in swaddling clothes, lying in a manger" (Luke 2:10-12 KJV).

There had never been and still has not been anything like this divine pronouncement to the Earth. Naba was reveling in the Glory of Abba's presence when Holy Spirit tapped him on the shoulder many times and, finally, had to knock Naba off his feet to get him to notice that the Host was ascending. I, Gabriel, had departed, the shepherds were scampering toward town with a little sheep in tow, and finally, Dutimus was endeavoring to catch up with them all. Naba regained his composure and zipped after him, not to miss Dutimus' big moment. "I," interrupted Naba, "had just had mine."

Seeing that this was a good moment to stop the story, for now, Naba addressed the little mouse. With a conspiratorial grin and wink to Gabriel, he said, "And now, little Gideon, let me direct you to your mansion." Gideon's eyes grew big as he began to take in the sights and sounds of his new world, and Naba explained that a favorite activity in all of heaven was the in-person, so to speak, telling of the resident's own stories. In this fashion, Naba inquired about Gideon's mighty-warrior-moments and how he had become acquainted with Mary, blessed among all women. As Gideon shared some of his story about how he had befriended Mary, Naba also continued to share more. As the two walked along, with Gabriel in tow, Naba smiled and said, "Let me tell you the rest of Dutimus' story on the way to your mansion. You can meet him yourself one day. And share your adventures with him as well.”

Final Conclusion

In Truth, It's All About the Baby. The stories in this novel, whether about the people surrounding Jesus' birth or what may have gone on with some animals who were part of the story, have come from our imaginations and our understanding of scripture. It is fascinating to imagine what may have been part of the events and actions of those involved in this event that changed the world. My hope is that you consider the stories a bit of fun and "what ifs" about the animal and heavenly kingdom.

Following the style of the Part I end-of-chapter questions and conclusions, I have added questions for Part II. The questions are: Have you encountered Jesus? Or is this the first time you are hearing about him? Do you want to know more before trying to draw conclusions about these stories, as Shirley suggests in Part I of this novel?

From my personal experience, I can tell you that Jesus is a very real person and, at the same time, is our very real savior and the son of God. The simple graphic below depicts Jesus' response to the separation of God and Man. If you are curious and want to learn more about Jesus' life story and his plan of salvation, a good place to begin is by reading the Gospels, the first four books in the New Testament of the Bible—Matthew, Mark, Luke and John.

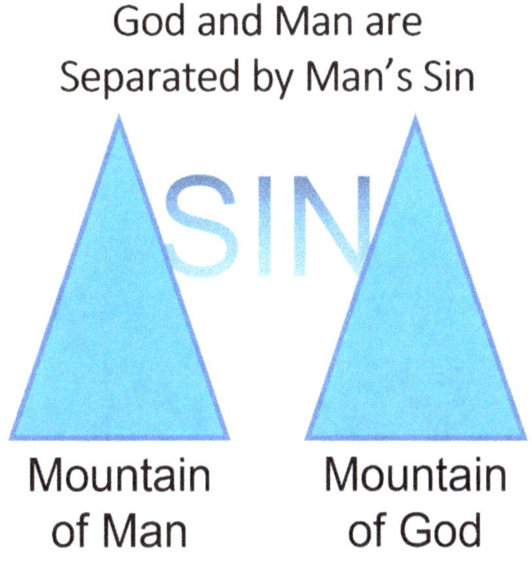

About the Authors

Part I: "What Child Is This?"

Shirley Farley is a retired missionary who spent thirty years living and teaching Bible stories to people from a West African country.

Shirley says, "my last year as a missionary was spent in Paris, France, still teaching diaspora West Africans. It was my joy to share stories from God's Word. Spending so much time sharing and studying God's Word leads to thinking about  those often untold things of the people mentioned in the Bible stories. My multi-world view guides my imagination and understanding of what it may have been like to live in such a Biblical time. My feeling/caring personality leads me to imagine how these people felt and what they experienced; these stories are born from that.

The illustrations are mine. As you have probably guessed, I am not an artist, at least not yet. The pictures are not perfect, yet

I believe they perfectly depict how I expected the stories to look. If you know any of my relatives and look closely at some of the story characters, you might notice that a few of them resemble (if you use your imagination well) some of my relatives. I used their faces as my models, although most probably could not recognize themselves. And that may be for the best.

Today, I live with my mother and our two dogs. I work part-time as an administrative assistant and spend my spare time writing, teaching English as Second Language classes to West African women through zoom, teaching Sunday school occasionally, and spending time with friends.

Part II: "O Come Let Us Adore Him, The Companion Stories"

Billie Stultz is the younger sister of Shirley. Shirley says she is a gifted teacher, writer and proofreader. She is also a strong believer, and if you need a prayer warrior on your side, she is the one to call upon.

Billie says, "I have taught English and theatre on the mission field of the American high school and college for thirty-plus years. When Shirley asked me to read the first draft of the stories in this novel, I did it, naturally, with pen in hand. Teaching English for so many years has made it difficult to do otherwise. Tending, also somewhat naturally, toward sarcasm, I expressed my appreciation for her work and promptly began to hassle her about why there were no animals telling their version of the events. After all, there are sheep, sheep dogs, a donkey and camels that figure prominently into the events. And, of course, the retelling of the story must not leave out the heavenly host. I suppose as any self-respecting big sister would do, she turned my playful criticism back on me, saying she would not presume to try to get into animals' heads and speak for them; she would leave that for me. That was that."

The gauntlet was thrown down and thus Part II was born. I hope you enjoy the reading as I did the writing.

Aside from teaching, and now it seems writing animal stories, I am a proud wife of thirty-nine years, mother of two and grandmother of three. My current goal is retirement in a few years so I can spend more time with my husband, children, and amazing grands.

About SGBLit

The name and logo stands for Shirley, Gail and Billie Literature. This novel, *In Truth, It's All About the Baby*, is our very first publication. Please check our website at SGBLit.com and our Facebook page at **SGBLit Books – Shirley Farley**. Both are available and are currently works in progress. When complete, these platforms will contain information on ordering books as well as plans for future projects such as audio and children's versions of this book and similar Biblical historical fiction.

> *'The Lord bless you and keep you; The Lord make His face shine upon you, and be gracious to you; The Lord turn His face toward you and give you peace"* (Numbers 6:24-26 NIV).

www.SGBLit.com
billie@sgblit.com
shirley@sgblit.com

www.ingramcontent.com/pod-product-compliance
Lightning Source LLC
Chambersburg PA
CBHW071158300726
48975CB00004B/1201